Praise for Gabriel Fitzmaurice's Poems for Children

'Gabriel Fitzmaurice qualifies as a minor legend'

Alan Murphy, *Inis*

'Ireland's favourite poet for children'

Claire Ranson, *Best Books!*

'We are in the domain of a poet who understands exactly what children are interested in, and the many dilemmas they face. As the poet himself says: "If you can't laugh or cry at these poems, you're OLD!". And he's right.'

Enda Wyley, *Recommended Reads 2012*

'Silly poems and serious poems, nice poems and naughty poems, with numerous echoes of the real world of home, school, children and parents'

Robert Dunbar, *The Irish Times*

Will You Be My Friend?

New and Selected Poems

for the Young and Young at Heart

First published in 2016 by
Liberties Press
140 Terenure Road North | Terenure | Dublin 6W
T: +353 (1) 405 5701|E: info@libertiespress.com |
W: libertiespress.com

Trade enquiries to Gill
Hume Avenue | Park West | Dublin 12
T: +353 (1) 500 9534 | F: +353 (1) 500 9595 |
E: sales@gillmacmillan.ie

Distributed in the United Kingdom by
Turnaround Publisher Services
Unit 3 | Olympia Trading Estate | Coburg Road | London N22 6TZ
T: +44 (0) 20 8829 3000 | E: orders@turnaround-uk.com

Distributed in the United States by
IPM | 22841 Quicksilver Dr | Dulles, VA 20166
T: +1 (703) 661-1586 | F: +1 (703) 661-1547 |
E: ipmmail@presswarehouse.com

ISBN: 978-1-910742-45-7
2 4 6 8 10 9 7 5 3 1

A CIP record for this title is available from the British Library.

Cover design by Karen Vaughan at Liberties Press
Illustrations by Karen Vaughan
Internal design by Liberties Press

Will You Be My Friend?

New and Selected Poems

for the Young and Young at Heart

Gabriel Fitzmaurice

For Katie and Paddy

With love from Grandad

Acknowledgements

Acknowledgements are due to the following,
who first published many of these poems
in the following collections:

The Kerryman, Tralee

The Moving Stair, 1989

Poolbeg Press, Dublin

The Moving Stair (enlarged edition), 1993
But Dad!, 1995
Puppy and the Sausage, 1998
Dear Grandad, 2001
A Giant Never Dies, 2002
The Oopsy Kid, 2003
Don't Squash Fluffy!, 2004

Mercier Press, Cork

I'm Proud to Be Me, 2005
Really Rotten Rhymes, 2007
G.F. Woz Ere, 2009
Do Teachers Go to the Toilet?, 2010
Splat!, 2012

Contents

From *The Moving Stair*

It's Only Simple Adding	15
The Moving Stair	17
The Teacher	19
An Only Child	20
Pension Day	21
The Mam	22

From *But Dad!*

Spider	24
How High?	24
An Apple for the Teacher	25
Santa Claus	26
Beebla	27

From *Puppy and the Sausage*

Daddy's Belly	34
A Goodnight Kiss	35
Her First Flight	36
Luddle-Uddle-Uddle	39
Nora	39
Will Grandad Die?	40
In Memoriam Danny Cunningham	40
I'd Like to Be	41

At the Seaside 42
Homework 43

From *Dear Grandad*

My Rainbow 44
Now We Are Eight 45
My New Blue Knickers 47
Dinner 48
The Land of Counterpane 49
Moan 50
My Best Friend 51
Dear Grandad 54
A Poem for Grandad 56
Hallowe'en 57
Grammar 58
What's a Tourist? 58
Learning the Tin Whistle 59
The Part of Mary in the Christmas Play 61
Running Away 63
In the Attic 64

From *A Giant Never Dies*

Saturday Night 65
The Parcel 66
Tomato Sandwiches 67
Bursting Pimples 68
The Well 69

From *The Oopsy Kid*

Daddy Is Married a Very Long Time   71
Head-Over-Heels   73
Grandad   74
Prayer   75
Shampoo   77
S   78
The School Tour   79

From *Don't Squash Fluffy!*

Imagination   81
Pooh   81
I'd Like to Be a Wrestler   82
Splat!   83
At the Zoo   84
The Dreamer   86

From *I'm Proud to be Me*

The True Story of Little Miss Muffet   87
Diarrhoea   87
A Hug   88
Dog's Pooh on Daddy's Shoe   89
The First Christmas   90
Happy Christmas!   91
I'm Proud to Be Me   92
Friends   93
When Tommy Fell into the Bin   94
English Spelling   95
A Letter to the Teacher   96
An Answer to My Prayer   97

Sitting with My Rabbit 98
Shopping with Mammy 99
In Summer 100
Middle Age 101
As Time Goes By 102
A Letter to Grandad 103
Poems for Lonely 104

From *Really Rotten Rhymes*

A Cross Boy 105
Belly Buttons 106
Dreamy Thomas 107
Do Teachers Fart? 108
Kissing on the Telly 109
Something Attempted, Something Done 110
Strimming the Garden 111
When You Make a Smelly 112

From *G.F. Woz Ere*

A Boy and his Dog 113
Messin' Around 115
A Teddy's for a Lifetime 117
Basher 119
Little Timmy Perfect 121
Puppy Love 122
My Picture's Crap 124
Birthday Party 125
Popularity 126

Different   128
I'm Special   129
Art   131
Mural   133
The Good Shepherd   134
Bored   136
Hygiene   137
The Race   138
ASBO   140
A Boy I Know   142
Our New Teacher   144

From *Do Teachers Go to the Toilet?*

Mary Had a Little Lamb   146
Slurry   146
Toilet Paper   146
The Singer   147

New Poems

Talking Horse   148
My Imaginary Friend   150
A Little Girl Visits . . .   151
Chasing the Rainbow   153
First Day at School   155
School Tour   156
A Young Child Learns to Write   157
New Words for Old   157
Fluffy Licks Our Horse's Poops   158

A Young Puppy Explores . . .   159
When the Car Killed Our Puppy   160
On the Death of Missy, Our Puppy   161
The Christmas Puppy   162
Carol   164
Christmas   165
Wetting the Bed   166
A Young Boy Discusses . . .   167
When Dan Got Diarrhoea in the Pool   168
In the Chipper   169
Tongue-twisters   170
Lonely Day   171
Will You Be My Friend?   171
Hush-a-Bye Baby   172
Nanas   172
Katie and the Dolphin   173
A Baby Brother for Katie   175

It's Only Simple Adding

It's only simple adding,
That's all you've got to do:
Just write the sum and add it –
It's just like 2 + 2.

That's fine for you to say it,
But you have no regard –
I think that you've forgotten
When 2 + 2 was hard.

The Moving Stair

The first time I went to Limerick
We went into this big store,
They had tons of things for grown-ups
On the bottom floor.

And Mammy went to sample
All sorts of perfume there
When, just below the counter,
I saw this moving stair.

So I jumped upon it
With a spaceman kind of hop
And up, up, up I floated
But the stair just wouldn't stop.

And then when I had gotten up
I felt a proper clown
For the stair just kept on moving –
How was I to get down?

And then it dawned upon me
That I was alone and lost
And I was small and frightened
And Mammy would be cross.

So then, I suppose you've guessed it,
I let out such a roar
That Mammy dropped the perfume
Down on the bottom floor;

And Mammy, she came for me
And I wasn't lost at all,
But that was quite a while ago
When I was young and small.

The Teacher

I kinda like the teacher
But he's most awful cross,
He really throws his weight about,
He sure can act the boss.

But still, he tells us stories
And he's nice and funny too,
He's nice – but he could be nicer.
I suppose we could be nicer too.

An Only Child
for Aoife Byrne

Oh, they'll say you're pampered
And they'll say you're spoiled
But *I'll* tell you one thing –
It isn't easy being an only child.

When you've brothers and sisters
You're never alone
But who's going to play with me
When *I'm* at home?

And when Mam and Dad are cross at me
I get all the blame;
I've no brothers or sisters
To share the pain.

I suppose, to be honest,
I have more toys
Than many of the other
Girls and boys.

But I wish I had a brother
Or a sister, or both;
Life would be much better fun,
And that's the truth.

Pension Day

Nan brought me to the village
To get her pension paid
Then she brought me to the pub
To get some lemonade –

At least that's how she said it:
She bought a pot of tea
And crisps and buns and doughnuts –
And lemonade for me.

After we had finished
I said I'd like to play
A game of pool with Nana
(I always get my way

With Nana);
So we started to play pool
And Nana had to put me
Standing on a stool

So I could see the pool-balls;
I beat them with the pole
Then stood up on the table
And kicked them in the hole.

And then we went for shopping –
Something for our tea –
Cake and buns for Nana,
Lemonade for me.

The Mam

Evenings when I was very small
I always clutched a stick
To save myself from the monstrous Mam –
She really scared me stiff.

With a big brown coat
And a big brown hat
And a big brown message-bag
And a face that was neither snarl nor smile,
She scared me, that old hag.

And always about tea-time
My stick would go *Bang! Bang!*
As I beat the step outside our door
To keep away the Mam.

And Mammy used to ask me
Why I got so awful mad,
Then I'd promise not to kill her –
I'd just scare that wizened hag.

With a big brown coat
And a big brown hat
And a big brown message-bag
And a face that was neither snarl nor smile,
She scared me, that old hag.

But now I'm a little older
And a bit more sensible
And now I know for certain
She was not a hag at all

But a tired old tattered woman
Astray in mind and limb
And I'm sorry that my terror
Made me do such frightful things.

But the big brown coat
And the big brown hat
And the big brown message-bag
And the face that was neither snarl nor
smile,
Would scare a little lad.

Spider

Hairy spider on the wall!
John stiffens, John bawls;

Cool as you like while John fretted,
Nessa picked it up and ate it.

How High?

How high can I piddle?
Higher than the door?
But the piddle hit it halfways up
And dribbled on the floor.

I got a ball of tissue
And rubbed the floor till dry
And soaked it off the lino.
Wow! I can piddle high!

An Apple for the Teacher

'Bring apples to eat', the teacher said,
But me, I'd rather mush,
So I threw mine down the toilet
But the apple wouldn't flush.

It just kept bobbing like a ball
As the flush foamed all about,
So I put my hand in the toilet bowl
And took the apple out.

I washed it in the basin
So nobody would know,
Then dried it on my jumper
And gave it to 'Mister O'

(That's what we call our teacher).
He rubbed it once or twice
And then he ate my apple.
He said 'twas very nice.

Santa Claus

Santa Claus is coming
To the village hall,
I'm going to see Santa Claus
And I won't cry at all.

Hello Santa! This is me!
(Oh Dad, he's awful hairy!
Oh Dad, don't let him near me!
Oh Dad, he's awful scary!)

Santa Claus was here today
In the village hall –
He gave me crisps and lemonade
(All I could do was bawl).

Beebla
for John and Nessa

1

Beebla wasn't sure that he was born
(What was it to be born? He didn't know),
But his mother had been dying four or five times.
Beebla threatened God: 'Don't let her go –
   If You do, then I won't say my prayers;
   If You do, then I won't go to Mass.'
The priest came and anointed Beebla's mammy.
Next morning, Beebla boasted in his class:
'My mother was anointed in the night-time;
The priest came to our house, I stayed up late.'
Beebla was cock-proud of his achievement:
All the class was listening – this was great!

2

Beebla played with all the boys at playtime
(The girls were in the school across the way) –
They played football with a sock stuffed
           with old papers,
He'd forget about his mammy in the play.
But always at the back of all his playing,
He knew about anointing in the night,
     And, knowing this,
    there could be no un-knowing –
Nothing in the world would change that quite.

3

Beebla got a motor-car in London –
A blue one with pedals which he craved
(Beebla'd been in hospital in London,
And, coming home, he'd had to have his way);
So his daddy bought him his blue motor-car,
He drove it all the way out to the plane,
And touching down, cranky with excitement,
He squealed till he was in his car again.

4

He drove around the village, a born show-off;
He pulled into a funeral, kept his place,
And all the funeral cars, backed up behind him,
Couldn't hoot, for that would be disgrace!
He drove off from the chapel to the graveyard,
And, tiring, he pulled out and headed back;
When his mother heard about it,
she went purple
And grabbed for her *wallop-spoon* to smack;

5

But his daddy shielded Beebla
from her wallops–
They brushed across his daddy's legs until
His mother's rage fizzled to a token:
She shook the spoon,
and threatened that she'd kill
Him if he didn't mind his manners:
But Beebla went on driving, till one day
A real car almost hit him at the Corner:
For safety, they took his car away.
Beebla didn't cry or throw a tantrum –
He knew that but for luck he would be dead,
And at night-time, after kisses,
hugs and lights-out,
He started up his car inside his head.

6

Beebla got a piano once from Santa –
He ran down to the church on Christmas Day
Before his mammy or his daddy could
contain him
(He wanted all the crowd to hear him play).
And he walloped notes and pounded them
and thumped them
As 'Silent Night' became a noisy day,
But it was his noise, all his own and he
could make it –
It said things for him that only it could say.

7

And he stole into the church another morning
When all the crowd had scattered
home from Mass,
And he went up to the mic like Elvis Presley
But he only made an echo – it was off!
So Beebla went back home to his piano,
To the sound of what it is to be alone,
'Cos Beebla had no brothers or no sisters
And he often had to play all on his own.

8

Beebla was the crossest in the village –
He was not afraid of beast or man:
He'd jump off walls, climb trees,
walk under horses –
He did it for a dare; until the Wren,
When the Wren Boys dressed up
in masks and sashes
And came into your house to dance and play –
Beebla was excited at the Wren Boys,
He simply couldn't wait for Stephen's Day;
But when the Wren Boys came to
Beebla's kitchen,
Like horrors that he dreaded in his dreams,
He howled, tore off into the bathroom,
And hid behind the bath
and kicked and screamed.
His mother came and told him not to worry,
Brought Tom Mangan in to him
without the mask –
Tom Mangan was his friend,
worked in the creamery,
But today Tom Mangan caused his little heart
To pound inside his ribcage like a nightmare,
Was fear dressed up and playing for hard cash –
Tom would be his friend again tomorrow,
But today Beebla hung around the bath.

9

He ran away from school the day he started –
He ran before he got inside the door –
And his friends who'd brought
him there that morning
Couldn't catch him. But he'd no time to explore
The village that morning in December
Before Christmas trees were common,
or lights lit –
Beebla had to figure out his problem
And he wasn't sure how he'd get out of it.

10

He stole into his shop and no one noticed
(His daddy's shop – his mammy wasn't well)
And he hid beneath the counter
till Daddy found him:
'Oh Daddy, Daddy, Daddy, please don't tell
Mammy that I ran from school this morning –
The doors were big and dark,
the windows high;
And Dad, I ran from school this morning –
I had to – 'twas either that or cry.'
His daddy didn't mind, his mammy neither,
He stayed at home till Eastertime, and then
One morning he got dressed up,
took his schoolbag,
Brushed his hair, and went to school again.

11

Beebla would annoy you with his questions –
He wanted to know everything – and why:
Why he was, what was it to be *Beebla*,
And would his mother live,
or would she die?
And what was it to die? Was it like 'Cowboys',
Where you could live and die and live again?
Or would Mammy be forever up in heaven?
(Forever was how much times one-to-ten?)

12

This was all before the television,
About the time we got electric light,
Before bungalows, bidets or flush-toilets,
Where dark was dark,
and fairies roamed the night.
This story's a true story – *honest Injun!* –
You tell me that it's funny, a bit sad;
Be happy! It has a happy ending,
'Cos Beebla grew up to be your dad.

Daddy's Belly

Daddy got a belly,
It's very stickin' out
An' Mammy says he got it
From drinkin' too much stout.

Daddy's very cuddly –
He's like a teddy bear,
Safe an' soft an' spongy,
Curly kind of hair.

Daddy got a belly,
He's goin' on a diet –
Mammy said he better
An' Daddy said he try it.

Daddy got a belly
But soon he will be thinner
Drinkin' no more porter
An' eatin' lot less dinner.

Her First Flight

'I love you, Dad! I love you!
I love this massive plane –
It looks like a big fat pencil-case
(Aer Spain – is it, Dad? Aer Spain?).

'This aeroplane's exciting,
It's noise-ing up to go –
Will it drive as fast as you, Dad?
But, Dad, we're going slow.'

*'We're driving to our runway, dear,
And then we'll go real fast –
Faster than even I drive.'*
'Whee, Dad! Whee! At last!

'We're going really speedy,
When are we going to fly?
Wow! Up, up, up we go, Dad!
'Way up in the sky.

'What's happening to my ears, Dad?
They're funny – I can't hear
(Well, kind of); what you say, Dad?
There's something in my ears.'

'Suck a sweet, 'twill help you –
It's a good idea.'
'Who's Eddie, Dad? Eddie?'
'I said: it's a good idea.'

'Look at the clouds now, Nessa,
We're coming to them – just;
In a minute we'll be through them.'
'Dad, it's like they're made of dust –

'The clouds are awful dusty,
I can't see a thing –
Just dark outside my window.
Now what's happening?

'We're above the clouds! The sunshine!'
'Sit back now and relax.
It's three hours to Tenerife –
Let's have a little nap.'

'Daddy, we're not moving –
Look down at the sea:
It's not moving, we're not moving;
This is boring – I have my wee.
'Daddy, where's the toilet?
I'm bored with this oul' plane.
'Look out the window, Nessa –
Look down and you'll see Spain.'

'Daddy, where's the toilet?
Is there any on this plane?'
'OK, OK, I'll take you.'
'Daddy, we're over Spain . . .

'When I was at the toilet,
I made poops as well as wee –
Where did the poops go, Daddy?
The poops I made, the wee?

'Did they fall down on some Spanish man
'Way 'way down below?
Where did my poops go, Daddy?
Where did my wee-wee go?

'What's next after Spain, Dad?
Will we get our dinner soon?
This aeroplane's exciting.
How far up is the moon?

'Dad, my ears are popping –
Is everything all right?
Daddy, oops! I chewed my sweet,
I got such an awful fright.
'But it's OK now, Daddy –
It's just the plane going down.
Daddy, Daddy! Tenner Reef!
Dad, is this our town?'

Luddle-Uddle-Uddle

My baby brother has no teeth,
He can only nibble,
I can't make out a thing he says
Because he's talking scribble.

Nora

Nora sits in the old folks' home,
She's very old and all alone;
She doesn't even know her friends,
This is how the twilight ends.

Her mouth's a hole where once it smiled
On me and every little child,
Her eyes are open wide and stare –
She doesn't even know who's there.

But Grandad sits and holds her hands,
He says that Nora understands;
He sits like that an hour or more,
Sometimes her breath is like a snore;

She wears a thing to keep her head
From falling down before she's dead.
He sits beside her in a chair,
He doesn't talk, he just sits there.

Grandad sits and holds her hands.
Sometimes she looks and understands.

Will Grandad Die?

'Will Grandad die? He's getting old.'
(I hug my little son.)
'Oh, please don't say that he will die –
Don't children keep you young?'

In Memoriam Danny Cunningham
1912-1995

I take her to the funeral home –
She wants to see him dead;
She's not afraid – she rubs his hands
And then explores his head.

'He not wake up I rub him.
Look, Daddy! He not move.
Where Danny, Dad?' she asks me.
'*Danny's dead, my love.*'

'Where Danny, Dad?' she asks again,
Then suddenly it's clear –
'The old Danny in the box,' she says,
'The new one – he not here.'

I'd Like to Be

I'd like to be a fat, green snot
Snailing down your lip –
A silken, soupy, slimy snot
Dribble, dribble, drip!

You'd squelch me in through your front teeth,
Roll me 'round a bit
Then suck me back to shoot me out,
A swirling, swollen spit.

At the Seaside

When you paddle
In the sea
First you shiver
Then you pee
And the waves
That licked your toes
Suddenly
Fizz up your nose
And you stumble –
Oh the shock –
And you swallow water
Yock
But it's sweaty summer weather
And it's great fun altogether

Homework

The teacher's suspicious –
I got my sums right,
He doesn't believe that I did them last night;
He says that I copied, he tries and he tries
To force me to say that I'm telling him lies.
He blushes with temper and lets out a roar,
Marches me roughly out on the floor
And tells me by God!
that he'll get to the truth,
That he doesn't know
what's become of the youth.
He tells me I copied, and when I deny
He presses and presses till I start to cry,
Then speaks to me gently. I do as I'm bid –
He asks if I copied, and I say I did.

My Rainbow
for Anna McGuire

I made a rainbow of my crayons,
I took them from their pack –
There were greens and reds and yellows,
And I threw out the black.

For green's the colour of the grass
And blue is of the sky,
Yellow is the warm round sun
But black is when you cry.

Yellow is a daffodil
And blue is of the sea,
Green is all things growing
And black is not for me.

I gathered up a rainbow,
The promise of the rain –
Though clouds are black and sky is grey,
The sun will shine again.

Now We Are Eight

Dad, they called you 'Gabriel',
Dad, I wonder why –
'Gabriel's such a big name
For such a little boy.

Did they always call you 'Gabriel',
Dad, when you were small?
Or did your name get bigger
As you grew up? Do all

Our names get bigger, Dad,
When we grow up? You see
I'm not too sure when I grow up
That 'Nessa' will fit me.

My New Blue Knickers

I got new blue knickers
In a packet on a hook;
I'm wearing my new knickers -
Do you want to see them? *LOOK!*

I love my new blue knickers,
I'm proud as proud can be –
I can't wait to show my knickers.
EVERYBODY LOOK AT ME!

I got new blue knickers,
I'm proud as proud can be –
I'm ready, are you looking?
MY NEW BLUE KNICKERS – SEE!

Dinner

I'm sick of fancy cooking!
Mammy, you're a pro
But *please* for dinner give me
Something that I know

Like chops and spuds and vege-bells,
Stuff that I can eat,
And after dinner, Mammy,
Just ice-cream for a treat.

Some day, Mam, I'll eat Chinese,
Italian as well,
And you won't have to force me
And I won't have to smell

To see if I can eat it,
Mammy when I grow,
But *please* this evening give me
A dinner that I know.

The Land of Counterpane

When I am sick and in my bed
I play these games inside my head,
But very soon I'm bored, you see,
Then I get up and watch TV.

Oh! yes I know, in days of old,
When children did what they were told,
They stayed in bed all through the day
And made up games that they could play.

But don't you think that, now and then,
They'd turn back the counterpane
And tiptoe down to the settee
And flick through channels just like me
If, long ago, they had TV?

My Best Friend

My best friend was Grandad.
I used to stay at his house on Friday nights
And that was great fun.
He used to take me to the chipper
After the nine o'clock news
And he'd buy two cartons of curried chips
and two sausages
And we'd eat them in his kitchen during
The Late Late Show.
He used to come up to our house on
Sundays for dinner
And I'd always want to sit beside him
at the table.

I remember one Christmas
I had just got a snooker table.
Grandad came up for Christmas dinner
And I had asked everybody else to play with me.
They all said no, they were too busy.
Grandad was in the middle of setting the table
And I asked him to play and he said he would.
He came over
And I actually had to place
the balls for him
It was so long since he had played snooker!

Well Grandad was my best friend;
He was so kind.
He was just unique to me.
Like he didn't know much Irish
Because when he was young he hadn't much
time for school
(He had to help at home on the farm,
he said,
And at fourteen years had to
hire himself with farmers
Because he had thirteen brothers and sisters
And times were bad),
But I often did my Irish homework with him,
and he always ended up right.

I remember the day Grandad died.
It was March.
I can't remember the date.
He rang Mom and said he thought he was
having a heart attack.
We rushed down to his house –
We got there in two and a half minutes
And when we went in we found Grandad
lying on the floor moaning.
And then he just died.
And I was below in the room crying
And then Mom and Nessa and Dad started
crying too.

At the funeral parlour I forgot myself
And said 'I'm sitting beside Grandad'.
But Grandad was in his coffin.

He was dead.

It was fine until they closed the coffin
And then I knew I'd never see him again in
this life.

Goodbye, Grandad, my best friend.
Goodbye
Goodbye.

Adapted from a story written by my son John.

Dear Grandad

Dear Grandad,
I hope you are happy
Because we are very sad.
I wish you were here
Because I miss you so much.

At first I was angry
When you died.
I cried and cried.

I love you, Grandad;
I miss you.

Nessa says that God took you
To mind his garden in heaven,
To make new flowers grow
Like you do in your garden.

I don't know.
Well, Grandad,
It's time to face reality.
I'll plant flowers on your grave;
I know you'll like that.
Mammy and Daddy say they'll let me.

Grandad,
I hope you enjoy your immortality.
Twice today I saw you smile at me.
Goodnight, Grandad,
I miss you, miss you, miss you.
John.

A Poem for Grandad

I made a poem for Grandad,
Most of it is true
Except for bits and pieces –
Things we used to do,

The fun we had together,
I told it like it was,
The truth of me and Grandad;
I made up bits because

Grandad's now my story,
I imagine him to be
The things we did together
And little bits of me.

I made a poem for Grandad,
Grandad's five weeks dead,
Now Grandad is the story
I see inside my head.

Hallowe'en

It's Hallowe'en! We dead are seen!
Tonight's our night to act up mean;
Now mere mortals are afraid –
It's great to be dead!

We haunt them from beyond the grave,
Tonight we rollick, revel, rave,
Now mere mortals are afraid –
It's great to be dead!

For dead we are, but not tonight,
Petty mortals walk in light,
Oh! tonight they're all afraid –
It's great to be dead!

And the mortals pray, pray, pray
That the dead will keep away,
But they'll die too one by one
And they'll join us in the fun.

It's Hallowe'en! Rise up! Be seen!
Hear the children laugh and scream,
All masked up and not afraid,
Pretending to be dead.

Grammar

Ebenezer Egghead
Is such a clever fellow,
He *loves* to show off all he knows,
So much he needs to tell you.

He boasts about his grammar,
But once I caught him right:
I asked him which was more correct –
'The yolk of an egg *is* white'
Or 'The yolk of an egg *are* white'?

He looked at me disdainfully,
He's such a clever fellow;
'The yolk of an egg *is* white,' he snapped.

(The yolk of an egg is yellow!)

What's a Tourist?

'Children, what's a tourist?
Can anyone tell me now?'

'Please sir, a man with a camera
Taking photos of a cow!'

Learning the Tin Whistle

I'm learning the tin whistle –
I play it really fast –
But the tune just runs away from me
(In this race, I'm always last).

The more the tune runs onwards,
The faster I must play,
Till I run out of fingers
And the tune gets clean away.

Come back 'Peg Ryan's Polka',
'The Dawning of the Day',
'The Britches Full of Stitches',
Come back and let me play.

I'll play you soft and easy,
I'll practise day and night –
Oh please! Slow down and wait for me
Till the music comes out right.

I'll play you soft and easy
Till feet tap on the ground
And all the air is music
In my cylinder of sound.

Come back 'Peg Ryan's Polka',
Give me one more chance –
My notes will turn to music
When my fingers learn to dance.

The Part of Mary in the
Christmas Play

I got the part of Mary
In the Christmas play –
'Twas grand until I realised
I had no lines to say.

First the Angel came to me –
I had to bow my head
And look as sickly-sweet as pie.
I wish I'd lines instead.

Then I had to follow Joseph –
I had no lines to say
(Even the two dressed as the donkey
Got to bray);

But I had to follow Joseph,
Quiet as a mouse,
While he went from inn to inn
And house to boarding house.

Then I had to hold the baby
When the shepherds came to pray;
And the same again for the Wise Men.
I wish I'd lines to say.

Don't you think that Mary
Would get to say a word;
After all, *she* chose to be
The mother of the Lord!

Don't you think that such a woman
Would have more to do
Than look as sickly-sweet as pie,
Forever dressed in blue?

Don't you think that such a woman
Should have lines to say
Instead of being an extra
In the Christmas play?

Running Away

He's running away from his mammy,
He's running away from his dad –
He can't take any more, so he's leaving;
He's snivelling, he's snuffling, he's mad.

So he goes to his room in a fury
(Making sure that his daddy can see)
And fills up his bag with his teddies.
But Dad just sits, cool as can be.

And he slams the front door so they'll hear him
And he sobs as he walks down the drive
And he keeps looking back towards
the window
To see if the curtains are moved.

Slowly he walks down the driveway –
Oh Daddy! Please call me back,
Oh Mammy! Come quickly and save me,
I'm sorry now that I packed.

And he stops at the gate and he wonders
Just where do I think I am going?
And Daddy comes out and he hugs him –
It's good not to feel so alone.

'Son, where did you think you were going?
We love you, we need you, you know.'
'Oh Daddy! Sure I was just bluffing.
Thanks for not letting me go.'

In the Attic

You're going up in the attic, Dad –
Please can I come too?
I'll even get the ladder, Dad,
And put it up for you.

Of all the places in our house
I love the attic best;
It's dark there – dark as Christmas,
With every box a chest

Of surprise and promise –
The things we store up there
Are put away like memories
To open if you dare.

You're going up in the attic, Dad –
Can I come up too, *please!*
For hidden in the attic
Among the memories

Is part of me and part of you –
The part we seldom show;
Oh, up there in the attic, Dad,
Is all we're not, below.

Saturday Night

Rub-a-dub-dub
Look what's in the tub!
Little Boy Blue with his horn,
Little Bo Peep
Who's lost all her sheep
(No wonder she looks so forlorn);

Little Jack Horner
In from the corner,
Little Miss Muffet's there too –
It's Saturday night
And they're scrubbed till they're bright
By the Woman Who Lives in the Shoe.

The Parcel

My name for it was 'parcel'
(Pooh-poohs in my pants),
And when you had to walk with it,
You made a kind of dance

With a wiggle and a waggle
And a sideways kind of glance,
Going home to Mammy
With a parcel in your pants.

And all the village noticed
By the funny way you'd walk,
And you had to brave the gauntlet
Of the whistles, squeals and squawks;

And even your friends would tease you,
Hold their noses, cry 'The stink!'
Till you got home to Mammy
And she'd wash you at the sink.

And she'd put you in new trousers
And advise you once again
To be sure and use the toilet
Before you went out with your friends.

Tomato Sandwiches

Soggy tomato sandwiches
Are the ones that I like best –
You can keep your biscuits,
Crackers and the rest.

I make them in the morning
Before I go to school
And when I've finished making them
I soak them in the pool

Of tomato juice upon the plate
So they go soft and pink –
They're soggy and they're juicy!
I really *really* think

That there's nothing in this world as nice
As a sandwich made this way –
And the best of all about it is:
I'm having some today.

Bursting Pimples

Did you ever burst a pimple?
It doesn't hurt at all –
The white stuff shoots right out of it
To the mirror on the wall;

And then you get a tissue
To mop up bits of blood
And you flush it down the toilet
And it goes off with the flood.

And you polish up the mirror
To get rid of all the goo
And you flush *that* down the toilet
Too.

Oh! I love bursting pimples!
It doesn't hurt at all
When all the bad inside you
Is splattered on the wall.

The Well

I heard it of a winter's night
In childhood, long ago,
When tales were told to keep the cold
Outside with the wind and snow

How once upon a moonlit night
A piper passed this way
Coming from a *céilí*
In the parish of Athea

And as he walked, he whistled
A tune, a merry tune,
And the only other sound that night
Was howling at the moon.

He walked along the fairy path,
Whistling his merry tune,
When suddenly a darkness
Stole across the moon

And all the dogs fell silent
As he came upon the well
And a voice from the waters spoke to him
And this is what befell:

There's some call it glaucoma
And some the fairies' curse
For when he woke next morning
Beside the fairy bush

He was blind; and ever after
He would never tell
What the voice of the waters whispered
From the fairy well.

The fairies are no longer
And all their wanton harm
And the well supplies fresh water
Piped up to a farm,

And when I ask the old man
Who told the tale to me
If he believes in fairies,
He says, 'I don't believe

In fairies'
And turns to face me then –
'No! I don't believe in fairies
But I'm afraid of them.'

Daddy Is Married a Very Long Time

Daddy is married a very long time,
His skin is out over his ring;
When he got married, it fitted him well,
'Cos back then my daddy was thin.

Daddy is married a very long time –
You don't need much brains to see that;
When people are married a very long time
They do things on their own and get fat.

Head-Over-Heels

She loves to go head-over-heels,
She loves to go head-over-heels,
She's more often found
With her legs off the ground
'Cos she loves to go head-over-heels.

She loves to go head-over-heels,
She loves to go head-over-heels,
With her legs in the air
And her head on the chair
'Cos she loves to go head-over-heels.

She loves to go head-over-heels,
She loves to go head-over-heels,
The world, she's found,
Is as good upside-down
'Cos she loves to go head-over-heels.

She loves to go head-over-heels,
She loves to go head-over-heels,
And she looks up at you
With a different view
'Cos she loves to go head-over-heels.

Come on, let's go head-over-heels,
Come on, let's go head-over-heels,
Don't mind what they'll say,
It's great fun, let's play!
Come on, let's go head-over-heels.

Grandad

for John

When people think of grandads,
They think of rocking chairs
And woolly rugs and slippers
And baldy wisps of hair.

That wasn't like my grandad,
He always seemed so young –
Though he was eighty years and more,
He loved to mix among

People who were younger,
He never acted old,
And you knew he'd always love you
Even when you were bold.

Yes! Grandad was as young as me
In many, many ways,
And now he's dead, I think of him
And all the nights and days

He minded me and made me feel
Just like a small boy should
For life with him was happy,
And life, like him, was good.

Prayer

In the deepest
Dark of night
When the moon is barking
And dogs are bright
And nothing is
As nothing seems
And all my dreams
Are dreaming dreams
And I don't know
That I'm asleep
And night things howl
And prowl and creep
May I go safely
Through the deep
In the dark of night
When I'm asleep.

Amen.

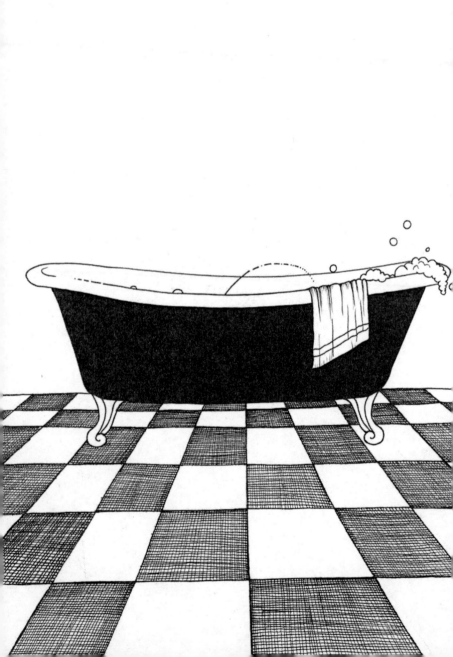

Shampoo

When I sit in the hot water,
I make wee-wees in the bath
And no one knows I've done it
But I don't worry about that.

And it's great to play with soap-suds
And do *splishy-splashy* there
And you forget you've made your wee-wees
Till it's time to wash your hair

And Daddy gets out the shampoo
And it's too late to cry
That there's wee-wees in the water –
It's in your ears and eyes,

It's running down your nose and mouth,
There's nothing you can do,
And Daddy says you've nice clean hair
When he's finished the shampoo.

S

When a word ends with an *s*
I get confused. Poor me!
Do I, or don't I (someone help!)
Put in an apostrophe?

Is it *its* or *it's*? (Please, someone help!)
My mind is in a mess –
I never know what I should do
With a word that ends in *s*.

In or out? (Please, someone help.)
This *s* thing sure annoys,
I'm sure some egghead thought it up
To pester girls and boys

(Or is it girl's and boy's?). Oh God!
It's worse than learning chess.
I'll never know what I should do
With a word that ends in *s*!

The School Tour

I've been on tour to Dublin
But I'd been there before;
I've been on tour to Kerry –
Been there. Done that. A bore!

Anywhere the teacher
Suggests we go on tour,
Someone is bound to say
'But I've been there before.'

School tours are so boring
When you've been everywhere,
But today the teacher told us
(Boy! I sat up in my chair)

That this year's tour was going
'Round our village – nowhere else;
He said that we know nothing
Until we know ourselves.

So off we walked in threes and twos
Around the village where
We thought that we knew everything.
We had to stand and stare

As teacher told us what he knew
About our native place –
It came alive in stories
And in the teacher's face;

And suddenly we realised
That because of this short tour
We were seeing our native place
As we'd never seen before.

The teacher led us back to school,
Wiped his sweating brow
And said, 'Yes! Worth the doing.
Ye can go to Dublin now!'

Imagination

I magination is the thing that
M akes you magic
A nd
G ives you
I nspiration to make everything
N ew,
A nd
T o
I nvent things that are
O nly seen by you, where
N othing is impossible. Imagine!

Pooh

'Does pooh always come from your bottom?
Mammy, I *need* to find out.
I hope it just comes from your bottom.
I'd *hate* if it came from my mouth.'

I'd Like to Be a Wrestler

I'd like to be a wrestler
With tree-trunks for my thighs,
My hands as big as shovels,
Volcanoes for my eyes!

And if I was a wrestler
I'd be the JCB
For that's what they'd all call me.
Oh my! The things you'd see –

You'd see me lifting wrestlers
And throwing them around
And sitting down upon them
When I had them on the ground;

I'd jump on them and throw them
Out of the wrestling ring,
And when I am the champion
(Just think of it!) I'll bring

My belt back home to Mammy
And she'll be proud of me,
And then she'll know her little girl
Has become the JCB.

That's me!

Splat!

It didn't come from outer space
(If it did, I wouldn't care) –
Oh no! it was much worse than that
When a bird pooped on my hair.

I was minding my own business,
Playing in the yard,
When I felt this *plop* upon my head,
Catching me off guard.

When I reached up to investigate,
I felt this sticky goo,
And all my friends were laughing
That my hair was stuck with pooh;

And then I started crying –
I cried most bitterly
That of all the places that pooh could land,
It had to land on me.

And I wouldn't let them wash me –
Oh Lord! it wasn't fair
So I just sat and sulked and sobbed
That a bird pooped on my hair.

I just sat and sulked and sobbed
That a bird pooped on my hair.

At the Zoo

Last year on our school tour
We all went to the zoo.
We spent the whole day up there;
There were lots of things to do.

We saw camels there and crocodiles
And snakes and parrots too,
And bears, a hippopotamus
And a baby kangaroo.

We went into the monkey house –
We went in there with glee
'Cos we all love the monkeys
(They're great fun, you see);

I went over to the monkey cage
To have a closer look
When a monkey piddled in my eye –
Oh boy! what rotten luck.

The monkey just came over
And piddled in my eye
And I had nothing but my sleeve
To wipe it dry

And I cursed that cheeky monkey
And I cursed the silly zoo
But my friends all started laughing
And I started laughing too
(What else could I do?)

Yes! I started laughing with them,
But until the day I die
I won't forget the monkey
That piddled in my eye.
No! I won't forget the monkey
That piddled in my eye.

The Dreamer

I play with all my classmates
But I've got no special friend –
No one likes me that much,
They all leave me to fend

For myself when school is out
So I just play alone,
Imagining all sorts of things
In our backyard at home.

And Mammy and Daddy ask me
Why I don't have friends to play,
But I just smile and tell them
It's OK.

'Cos the games that I am playing
Are not like other games
(Games like those we play at school,
Bound by rules and names)

And I can play them anywhere
'Cos all I have to do
Is find a quiet space in my mind
And let the dreams come through.

The True Story of Little Miss Muffet

Little Miss Muffet
Sat on a spider
(He couldn't get away) –
He went SPLAT!
She squashed him flat
And his guts came out like whey.

Diarrhoea

I had a queasy tummy,
I went up to the loo,
And when I'd done my business
I made pooh-juice instead of pooh.

And that's true.

A Hug

A hug is huge and happy,
It warms you through and through –
Even when you're lonely,
It makes you good as new.

A hug is huge and happy,
A hug is what you do
When you open up from inside out
And let your feelings through.

A hug is huge and happy,
A hug is always true –
It's just pretend when it's not meant,
'Cos a hug makes one of two.

Dog's Pooh on Daddy's Shoe

It wasn't mud or puddle
That stuck to Daddy's shoe,
Oh no! It was much worse than that –
It was pooh!

He was walking on the footpath,
He wasn't looking down,
Otherwise he would have seen
A lump of doggy's brown;

And Daddy stepped right in it
And it stuck on to his shoe
And even though he wiped it off
You still could smell the pooh
From his shoe.

That's true!

The First Christmas

Was there a smell from the cow in the stable?
Did the ass rise his tail up and bray?
Was there animals' poops 'round the manger
In Bethlehem that Christmas Day?

Did the sheep keep quiet for the shepherds?
Was the baby able to play?
Did his mother croon when she burped him
In Bethlehem that Christmas Day?

Did Joseph know how to change nappies?
And the angels – did they fly away?
If I was about, I'd have sussed all that out
In Bethlehem that Christmas Day.

Happy Christmas!

Christmas is a postcard
With sleigh-bells in the snow,
Christmas is a movie
Where Santa beams 'Ho! Ho!'
Christmas is a season,
And when it comes each year
'It's not a bit like Christmas'
Is what you'll likely hear.
So you try to buy back Christmas
No matter what the cost,
Christmas is an open cheque,
A childhood that is lost.
Christmas is the Santa Claus
In every human heart,
The part that gives unbidden,
The sacred, selfless part.

Happy Christmas!

I'm Proud to Be Me

Though you live in a house
With a proper address
And wear proper clothes
Not my hand-me-down dress,
Though you think that you're better
Than I'll ever be
And look down on our equals,
I'm proud to be me.

Friends

This little girl in Infants
Who came to school last week
Was crying in the yard at play
'Cos a ball banged off her cheek.

The teacher crouched beside her,
Kind as kind could be,
And asked would someone mind her
And I said, 'Please, Miss, me.'

The teacher said to mind her
And I said I would
'Cos I have a little brother
And I mind him very good.

So I put my arm around her
(She was crying very hard)
And off we went together
For a walk around the yard.

And as we walked together,
My hand around her still,
She asked me would I be her friend
And I said, 'I will.'

And then – well . . . she got better
And she wasn't crying at all
And teacher said the big boys
Should be careful playing ball.

That's all!

When Tommy Fell into the Bin

The Infants were out in the toilets
And whatever way Tommy came in
(How did he manage to do it?),
Tommy fell into the bin.

I don't know how he managed to do it –
He was walking quite normally in,
Drying his hands with a tissue,
When Tommy fell into the bin.

He fell in like a sack of potatoes
And everyone saw him fall in –
It took Mrs Strong to extract him
When Tommy fell into the bin.

He fell in like a sack of potatoes
And only that Tommy is thin
He'd be stuck down inside there forever
When Tommy fell into the bin.

He would.

When Tommy fell into the bin.

English Spelling

English spelling is tough
And can leave a poor kid in a hough –
It's fine when you taulk
But at spelling you baulk
'Cos that's when the words call your blough!

A Letter to the Teacher

Dear teacher,

My Johnny came home from school today –
I know he called Mike Cullen names and knocked
him down at play;
And I know he pulled Trish Coady's hair and lifted
up her skirt
And swung off Tommy Purcell's back and tore his
new school shirt.
And so I would appreciate if you would tell those
three
To keep away from Johnny or they'll hear from me,
For Johnny wouldn't touch them unless he was pro-
voked
(I know he provokes his schoolmates but it's only
as a joke).
Please move Tommy, Mike and Trish from sitting
near my son
(When he comes home this evening, he'll tell me if
it's done)
For although he gets in trouble, Johnny's not at
fault,
And if I meet those upstarts, they'll soon be called
to halt.
I believe in rearing children; my belief in this is
strong.

I remain, yours sincerely,

Mrs Mine-Are-Never-Wrong

An Answer to My Prayer

Mammy died a year ago
And I was only five;
Daddy and I wanted
Mam to be alive

But she's alive in heaven,
I talk to her at night,
Because I say my prayers to her
That we will be all right.

And suddenly this morning
I woke up at dawn,
I hopped into Daddy's bed,
He woke up with a yawn.

I said 'Good morning, Daddy,
Let's have a cup of tea',
We went into the kitchen
And he made tea for me.

We drank our tea together
Myself and Dad,
Just to be beside him
Made me glad,

And as the morning brightened
And although we had been sad,
I hugged and kissed my Dad and said
'Aren't we very happy, Dad?'

Sitting with My Rabbit

All the sun-long summer,
When I have time to spare,
I sit with my rabbit
In an easy chair.

She sits there black and shiny,
Soft and silky sleek,
Her ears relaxed upon her back,
Her whiskers to my cheek.

I rub her, rub her, rub her,
For I just love to feel
Her, cuddly as a teddy,
Except that she is real.

She sits upon my belly,
Her head upon my chest,
Brown eyes wide, unblinking,
The rabbit I love best –

Magic!

Shopping with Mammy

Shopping with Mammy
Is a definite *no*,
She may have been cool
But 'twas long, long ago,

For the things that she says
Would look good on me
I just couldn't bear
My buddies to see;

It even makes uniforms
Not look so bad –
Next time, I think,
I'll go shopping with Dad

For he doesn't care
Whatever I pick,
No, he doesn't care,
Just as long as I'm quick,

But shopping with Mammy
Is a definite pain;
I'll never go shopping
With Mammy again.

(Until the next time.)

In Summer

Just me and my friend Jessie
Sitting on the grass;
All the sun-long summer
We watch the world pass.

Just me and my friend Jessie
Sitting real slow
On the ditch outside our driveway
With the radio.

We listen to it sometimes
But mostly we just laze
And listen to the buzzing
And flutter of the days,

The lazy days, the hazy days
We hope will never end,
Just sitting on the roadside,
Me and my best friend.

In summer.

Middle Age

When the world is going to pieces
And all your friends agree,
When the onslaught never ceases
And everywhere you see

Children being children
And you feel that you should scold,
Daddy, I've got news for you –
You're getting old!

As Time Goes By

When I was young, oh! years ago,
My daddy was so cool
I'd borrow his CDs and tapes
To show my friends at school.

But, now I'm older, things have changed,
I no longer borrow his –
When Daddy wants to see what's cool,
He borrows my CDs.

For people change like music
And as time goes by
I'm no longer just a follower,
Daddy's little boy;

I'm no longer just a follower,
Dad trusts me now to know
What's going on in music
Like he knew long ago.

I'm growing up like music,
He borrows my CDs
Where once, when I thought Dad was God,
I used to borrow his.

A Letter to Grandad

Dear Grandad,

Have you met Grandma in heaven?
You always believed that you would:
Though you were happy, you missed her.
(I know she'd meet you if she could.)

What's it like there in heaven?
There's only so much we can say,
Only so much we imagine,
A place where each tear's wiped away.

I hope you're happy in heaven,
Where God will make everything new –
That's what it says in the Bible,
But, Grandad, I so, so miss you.
I know what it says in the Bible,
But, Grandad, I so, so miss you.

John

Poems for Lonely

Most poems we learn are funny,
The kind you want to say
When you're feeling happy
With your friends at play.

But where are the poems, the other poems,
The ones that speak for you
When you're alone and lonely
And very, very blue?

Where are the poems for lonely,
The ones we need when we
Needs words to turn to,
Words of poetry?

We all need poems for lonely,
Words that say us true,
That light us in the darkness
As only poem-words do.

We all need poems for lonely
When we're full of care
'Cos nothing speaks from lonely
Like a poem-prayer.

No! Nothing speaks from lonely
Like a poem-prayer.

A Cross Boy

I'm a cross boy. I can't help it.
I get into trouble each day –
In trouble at home, in trouble at school,
For the things that I do and I say.

Then I thought of a plan to get better,
To keep me from trouble, and so
I opened my Mam's holy water
And drank the whole lot in one go.

I drank all my Mam's holy water
She'd brought in a bottle from Lourdes,
I drank all my Mam's holy water,
Hoping that I would get cured.

But no! I'm as crazy as ever,
My plan didn't work. Never could.
I thought I'd get better by magic
But it takes more than that to get good.

I'm a cross boy. I can't help it.
I get into trouble here still
But even cross boys can do better.
I can try to do better. I will.

Dreamy Thomas

Dreamy Thomas picks his nose –
He may not know it but he does,
Dreaming things that only he
In his wonderland can see.
He sticks his finger up his snout,
Turns his finger round about,
Turns it this way, turns it that,
Fills his nose up very fat,
And when he takes it out again
His nose goes back to being thin.
And all the while he's dreaming dreams
Where nothing is as nothing seems,
Dreaming poems in a world of prose,
While Dreamy Thomas picks his nose.

Dreamy Thomas.

Kissing on the Telly

Kissing on the telly
Makes me really sick,
Every time I see it
I get the remote and flick

To some other channel,
To football, racing, darts,
Kissing's just for sillies
Who draw these pink love-hearts

On every bit of paper
That they come across,
I'd ban kissing if I could,
And 'twould be no loss,

'Cos kissing's really stupid,
It makes me want to puke.
If there's kissing on the telly,
DON'T LOOK!

Something Attempted,
Something Done

This little boy in Infants
Can't wipe his bottom,
So he comes in to his teacher
(God bless the little tot)

With his trousers 'round his ankles
And says 'Please, Miss, will you
Wipe my botty-wotty
Because I made a pooh.'

So she takes him to the toilet
And shows him what to do
Now he can wipe his botty-wot
When he's in the loo.

Good man yourself!

Strimming the Garden

Did you ever swallow pooh?
Well, Daddy did.
It's true.

He was strimming the front garden,
He was singing a little song,
Singing a song to cheer himself
As he strimmed along.

Well anyway
He didn't see
The dog's pooh
When, gracious me!
The strimmer shot the pooh
Into Daddy's mouth,
And Daddy had it swallowed
Before he could spit it out.

He gargled, gargled, gargled –
Well, that's all you can do
(But it makes no difference)
When you swallow pooh.
He gargled, gargled, gargled,
And the next time he went out
Strimming the front garden,
Was Daddy singing?

No way!

He shut his mouth.

When You Make a Smelly

When you make a smelly,
What are you to do?
You act like all the others
And pretend it wasn't you.

When you make a smelly,
You hide it, so you do,
And hope no one will notice
The smelly came from you.

You do!

A Boy and His Dog

He played with me, I slept on him,
Those summers in the sun,
But now my dog is dying
And we have to put him down.

He played with me when I was young,
He was my greatest friend,
But now he's blind and dying.
This is the end.

Goodbye, old friend, I'll miss you,
We'll put you out of pain,
But I know I'll never, ever see
The likes of you again.

Goodbye, old friend, I'll miss you,
My childhood ends today,
The summers that I slept on you,
The games we used to play.

Goodbye, goodbye, dear Sandy,
I'll hold you to the end,
I'd swap all other dogs for you,
My bestest, bestest friend.

Messin' Around

Me and my best mate
Always can be found
When we get together
Just messin' around.

No one to bother us,
To hurry or to hound,
Just me and my best mate
Messin' around.

Messin', messin', messin',
We're always to be found
When we get together
Messin' around.

No chores to do, no lessons,
Those things to which we're bound,
Just me and my best mate
Messin' around.

And when the world's on top of me
And I can't get off the ground,
All I do to get me through
Is messin' around.

Messin', messin' messin',
One thing I have found,

That's to lose the blues you just must
choose
Messin' around.

To lose the blues you just must choose
Messin' around.

OH YEAH!

A Teddy's for a Lifetime

A teddy's for a lifetime,
Not just for childhood years,
The one you take to bed with you,
Who keeps you from your fears.

A teddy's for a lifetime,
Even when you're old
You still can hold your teddy
When you've nothing else to hold.

A teddy's for a lifetime –
Like the one I saw today
In the old folks' nursing home
Held by a little grey-

Haired smiling lady
Who fed her birthday cake
To her tattered, trusted teddy;
I watched her, trembling, break

Her cake into bite sizes
And give her teddy half
And, even though 'twas funny,
No one laughed

When she fed her teddy
Like she did, a little child,

The last thing to hold on to
Now she's far out in the wilds.

Her teddy.

Basher

Basher is a bully,
He thumps me, calls me names,
Always wants to be the boss
At lessons and at games.

Basher is a bully,
I get headaches, so I do,
I get headaches every morning
Before I go to school

'Cos Basher always bullies me
And makes my life so hard
But I can't keep away from him
In class or in the yard;

No, I can't keep away from him
Although I know I should,
And every time I play with him
It turns out no good.

No, I can't keep away from him
No matter how I try
'Cos I want him to notice me.
That's why.

I want him to notice me
And, when he does, it's great,
But mostly it's being bullied
And these headaches that I hate.

Mostly it's being bullied
In class and out at play.
I'll have to tell the teacher
And learn to keep away.

I'll have to tell the teacher
And learn to keep away.

I will.

Little Timmy Perfect

Little Timmy Perfect
Always does his best,
Must be first at everything,
Better than the rest.

It's fine when things go right for him,
But if he should make
Even the very
Tiniest mistake,

Timmy just can't take it,
He breaks down in a flood
Of bitter disappointment
And thinks that he's no good.

No! He just can't take it,
He must always be the best,
He'll have to learn that it's OK
To be like the rest.

He'll just have to learn
That we all mess up sometimes
But if we really love ourselves
It all works out just fine.
If we really love ourselves
It all works out just fine.
Thank God!

Puppy Love

1.

He asked me to go out with him
Out of the blue;
I've never had a boyfriend,
I don't know what to do.

He asked me to go out with him,
He took me by surprise,
He's skinny, tall and cheeky
But he's got lovely eyes.

He asked me to go out with him,
I said no, but still
If he asks me to go out again
I will.

2.

He asked her to go out with him
And she said she would,
But the Champ was very sweet on her
And now he's not so good;

He says he'll fight him in the yard
But that won't be much use
'Cos when he asked her to go out with him
She refused.

He asked her to go out with him,
That took some guts, oh boy!
I couldn't do a thing like that,
I'd be much too shy;

I couldn't do a thing like that,
I'd have to shut my mouth,
So I'll just play with the boys today
And let them fight it out.

I will.
I'll let them fight it out.

'My Picture's Crap'

'My picture's crap,'
I say to you,
Please, oh please!
Say it's not true.

'My picture's crap',
Oh please! Approve,
I need support,
I need love.

'My picture's crap',
Oh! Can't you see,
It's not the picture,
It's really me?

'My picture's crap',
Oh please! Please say
That it's all right,
That I'm OK.

'My picture's crap',
I say to you,
Please, oh please!
Say it's not true.

PLEASE!

Birthday Party

Noreen had a party,
She invited all the class,
They all got invitations,
But she passed

Me over. I got no card;
My classmates cheered with glee
When they got their invitations.
What's wrong with me

That I didn't get invited?
No one invites me;
I'm always, always left out.
I'd love to be

Invited to their parties
Like the other girls and boys;
Instead I have to stay at home
And play alone with toys.

I'd love to be invited;
My classmates cheer with glee
When they get their invitations,
But no one invites me.

What's wrong with me?

Popularity

I don't mind if I'm not popular,
Not if I have to do
Things that I don't want to,
Now I've thought it through.

I don't mind if I'm not popular,
Let the others laugh at me,
I don't think that it's important,
And popularity

Is for the ones who tease me
(They tease so they can show
Their friends that they don't want me);
Does it hurt me? No!

Although once it used to
And I wondered why,
But now I know I'm different
To the other girls and boys.

Yes, now I know I'm different,
But that's OK by me;
I've learned to accept myself,
And popularity

Is fine for those who need it
But I don't, now that I
Accept that I'm different
And no longer wonder why.

It's fine for those who need it
But I don't, now that I
Accept that I'm different
And no longer wonder why.

It's OK.

Different

I'm different so they tease me –
Can they not live with that?
Can they not live with difference?
I know what they're at.

They're afraid of being different,
Of being on their own,
There's security in numbers,
There's none when you're alone.

They're afraid of being different,
So they tease me all they can,
But I don't mind being different.
I am who I am.

I'm Special

I'm special. I'm adopted.
My parents wanted me;
Some children are not wanted,
And that's a tragedy.

I'm special. I'm adopted.
I wish every child could be
Treated like they're special,
The way my folks treat me.

I'm special. I'm adopted.
I'll do everything I can
To make each child feel special
When I am a man.

I will.

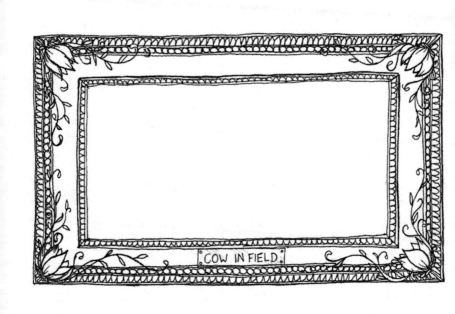

COW IN FIELD

Art

He told us to draw a picture
Of anything at all,
Some drew summer holidays,
Some drew playing ball,

Some drew friends and families,
A concert in the hall,
But I just sat and drew
Nothing at all.

And teacher came around to look
At the things we drew,
When he came to me he said,
'Mister Picasso, you

Haven't drawn anything,
You're really very bold,
Your sheet's blank, it's empty',
Then I upped and told

Him that it wasn't,
That 'twas a cow inside a field,
He said, 'But there's no grass there'.
Still I wouldn't yield.

I said the cow had eaten it
And the field was grassless now
And still he tried to best me.
He said, 'I see no cow.'

I looked him squarely in the eye
And bravely then I said,
'That's because it's milking time
And the cow is in the shed.'

But I knew he's never get it,
The teacher's just too old –
All he thinks of what I've said
Is that I'm being bold.

He said it wasn't funny,
That I was just being smart,
But that's the stuff that goes today.
My blank page is art!

Mural

We made a mural on the wall,
Picked out what we'd paint an' all –
An apple tree with apple hearts,
Faces you only see in art,
With no mouth or nose or eyes –
We drew 'em that way to surprise
People who can only see
Things as *they* think they should be,
People who would criticise
Instead of playing with their eyes,
Seeing things they've never seen.
We made 'em yellow, red and green,
And when we'd finished we signed our names,
Telling all we played this game,
The game where you will always be
What you are in what you see
On our school wall.
Our mural.

The Good Shepherd

He told us the story
Of the shepherd and his sheep,
How the shepherd in the story
Had a love so deep

For each and every sheep he had,
And how he'd leave his flock
And search the whole place over
If any sheep was lost.

He told us the story,
How the shepherd always cared
For each and every sheep he had
So we wouldn't be scared.

But then I took the story
Beyond what we were taught –
What happened to the sheep then?
How many sheep were caught

For mutton by the shepherd?
The story doesn't tell;
It has a happy ending,
And it's maybe just as well

To finish up all happy,
But what's a kid to do
With the teacher's happy ending
When you think it through?

For the poor sheep in the story
The shepherd minds so well
End up dead as mutton,
But the story doesn't tell.

The poor sheep in the story
The shepherd minds so well
End up dead as mutton.
The Bible doesn't tell.

Bored

Don't want to do no lessons,
Don't really want to play,
Sitting on the wall here,
It's a boring day.

Sitting with my friends here,
Bored as bored can be,
And it's no consolation
That they're as bored as me.

Sitting with my friends here,
On this boring wall,
Watching all the younger kids
Running, playing ball.

Sitting on the wall here
While all the others play,
Nothing to do and all day to do it,
It's a BORING day.

Hygiene

Young teenage boys in summer
Would knock you with BO –
Sweaty bodies, smelly feet –
But are they bothered? No!

They go on stinking, stinking
Until they chance to meet
The goddess of their fantasies,
Then they wash their feet

And lash on antiperspirant –
It only goes to prove
That, when it comes to hygiene,
There's no substitute for love.

The Race

I'm not a boy racer
But my girlfriend let me down
And went out with the coolest
Teenager in our town.

He wasn't a racer either
But when I passed them on the road
Driving to the disco,
The competition showed;

He passed me out, I passed him out,
Hoping to impress
The girl we both fancied.
Now things are in a mess.

We crashed, he's in a wheelchair,
My girlfriend is dead;
I escaped with minor injuries
But I'm messed-up in my head

'Cos I didn't mean to kill her,
I just wanted to impress,
Now I'll never, ever see her,
And everything's a mess.

I escaped with minor injuries,
I'm messed-up in my head,
I didn't mean to kill her,
I wish that I was dead.

I didn't mean to kill her.
I wish 'twas me instead.

Asbo

They're bringing in the ASBOs
To give the police more power,
The power to strip-search twelve-year-olds
They find at any hour

Hanging out with people,
The kind the police suspect
Even if they're innocent.
Such powers should be checked.

And if you get an ASBO,
It won't just go away;
You can't be a nurse in England
Or work in the USA;

You can't go to New Zealand
Or take a trip to Oz.
Your life is pretty limited,
And all of this because

They're bringing in the ASBOs,
A politicians' ruse
To show they're doing something.
(It looks good on the news.)

They're bringing in the ASBOs
And though I don't agree
With strip-searching twelve-year-olds
(Kids like you and me).
They're bringing in the ASBOs
And I'm a bit less free.

I am.

We're all a bit less free.

A Boy I Know

He rises every morning,
Gets up all alone,
No one up to wake him,
He does it on his own.

No one makes his breakfast,
They leave him cash instead
And he goes up to the local shop
To be fed.

A can of Coca-Cola,
A jumbo breakfast roll,
That's what he has each morning
On his way to school.

In school he gets in trouble
In class and out at play,
No lessons done, disrupting fun,
But he goes there every day.

I wonder why he bothers,
He could just stay in bed
All morning like his parents,
But he doesn't. No. Instead

He rises every morning,
Walks up to the school,
Knowing he'll be in trouble

When he acts the fool.

He gets up unlike the others,
I really don't know why,
He comes to school each morning,
But I admire this boy

Who rises undefeated
While his parents on the dole
Leave him to his cola
And a jumbo breakfast roll.

Our New Teacher

They blame him 'cos he's nice to us,
They say he's no control,
But it's the first time I've been happy
Since I came into this hole

'Cos he's not like other teachers,
He treats us just as we
Are, human beings like himself
With human dignity.

He treats us like we're human,
With freedom to express
What we're really thinking,
But this doesn't impress

The keep-them-down-at-all-costs
Anti-kids brigade
Who prefer to see us silent.
I think that they're afraid

Of things like fun and freedom –
What would the world be
If everybody, God forbid!
Was free?

If everybody, God forbid!
Was free, what would they do?
An end to all their privilege;
Freedom for the few.

So when our teacher shines a light
Into our pitch-black hole,
They whisper behind his back
That he's got no control.

They whisper behind his back
But there's no secrets in this town –
He knows the things they're whispering,
And it gets him down.

Someday soon he'll leave us,
Tired of all who would
In blind ignorance put down
The beautiful and good.

Someday soon he'll leave us
To meanness and 'control',
Defeated by his vision
And his gentle teacher's soul.

Someday soon he'll leave us
But he taught a kid like me
That the joy of education
Is learning to be free.

Someday soon he'll leave us
But he taught us to be free
And no one can take that away.

That's his legacy.

Mary Had a Little Lamb

Mary had a little lamb,
Each morning she would greet her,
And then one day the butcher came
And Mary got to eat her.

Slurry

I saw them spreading slurry, Mam –
'Twas worse than a smelly loo,
And, Mam, do you know what slurry is?
A tractor making pooh.

Toilet Paper

Don't ever use cheap toilet roll,
It's worse than bad. *How come?*
'Cos your finger goes right through it
And you stick it up your bum.

The Singer

The song opens
From the centre of my heart,
I am the song here,
I am the singer.

I sing my hope,
I sing my love,
I sing my light,
I sing my trouble.

In the corner of a public house
Alone, my back to the wall,
Instead of being a pop star
In theatre, park or hall,

In the corner of a public house
Singing for myself alone,
I am the singer here,
I am the song.

Talking Horse

Neigh-neigh, neigh-neigh, neigh-neigh,
neigh-neigh,
Neigh-neigh, neigh-neigh, neigh-neigh,
Neigh-neigh, neigh-neigh, neigh-neigh,
neigh-neigh,
I'm talking horse today.

Moo-moo, moo-moo, moo-moo, moo-moo,
Moo-moo, moo-moo, moo-moo,
Moo-moo, moo-moo, moo-moo, moo-moo,
I can talk cow too.

Bow-wow, bow-wow, bow-wow, bow-wow,
Bow-wow, bow-wow, bow-wow,
Bow-wow, bow-wow, bow-wow, bow-wow,
I can talk dog as well as cow.

Purr-purr, purr-purr, purr-purr, purr-purr,
Purr-purr, purr-purr, purr-purr,
Purr-purr, purr-purr, purr-purr, purr-purr,
I can talk fur.

Tweet-tweet, tweet-tweet, tweet-tweet,
tweet-tweet,
Tweet-tweet, tweet-tweet, tweet-tweet,
Tweet-tweet, tweet-tweet, tweet-tweet,
tweet-tweet,

I can talk bird-sweet.
Cock-a doodle, cock-a-doodle,
Cock-a-doodle-doo,
Cock-a doodle, cock-a-doodle,
I can rooster too.

For I'm a rooster, I'm a bird,
I'm saying creatures with these words,
A dog, a cow, a cat, a horse,
Talking animal in my verse,
For I am anything I say,
And I'm talking horse today.

Neigh, neigh.

My Imaginary Friend

My imaginary friend
Is with me every day,
When there's no one else around
We play;

She never, ever teases me,
Call me names or pulls my hair,
She's always there to be my friend
When no one else is there.

My imaginary friend
Is always good and kind;
I don't care if you insist
She's only in my mind

'Cos I can see and hear her,
Smell her, too, and feel.
Say what you like about her,
She's real.

Say what you like about her,
She's real as you and I,
And now I'm going to play with her.
Goodbye!

A Little Girl Visits Her Baby Brother's Grave
for Éabha Lawlee

I went to baby Mícheál's house
In the abbey, where
I picked a flower for Mícheál
And laid it there,

A little flower for Mícheál,
A daisy just from me,
And then I spoke to Mícheál
And I could see

Him listening as I spoke to him,
I told him all my news –
How I'm out of nappies now,
How I don't need to snooze

As often as I used to,
He spoke to me as well;
He told me all the secrets
That he will only tell

To me, his big sister,
And then we said goodbye,
And I went home with Mammy
And I didn't even cry

'Cos Mícheál has his own house,
And me and Mam have ours,
And I love to go to Mícheál's house
To see his lovely flowers.

I love to go to Mícheál's house
To see his lovely flowers.

Chasing the Rainbow

We set out for the rainbow's end
To find the crock of gold;
That's where the fairies keep it,
We were told;

We set out for the rainbow's end,
It was in Willie's lawn,
But when we got there,
It was gone;

'Twas gone as far as Paddy's field
'Way off down the lane,
But when we got to Paddy's field
It was gone again.

Every time we got to it,
'Twas nowhere to be found;
The fairies had moved it on
To some further ground.

And so we chased the rainbow
But it always got away;
In the end we had no gold
But we got to play

Chasing with the rainbow.
It was brilliant fun,
And you won't ever catch it,
No matter how you run.

No! You won't ever catch it,
No matter how you try,
But we had brilliant fun today,
Playing with the sky.

Yes! We had brilliant fun today,
Playing with the sky.

First Day at School
for Ella Hannon

I cried coming home from school,
I cried coming home from school –
I wanted to stay
With my new friends today,
So I cried coming home from school.

I cried coming home from school,
I cried coming home from school,
As I walked down the street
On the lonesomest feet,
I cried coming home from school.

I cried coming home from school,
I cried coming home from school,
But Granny and Dad
Said 'Don't be so sad,
You can go to school again tomorrow.'

Then I smiled coming home from school,
I smiled coming home from school,
For tomorrow we'll play
In school like today,
So I smiled coming home from school.

Hurrah!

School Tour
A Song

Stop the bus! I have a wee-wee!
Stop the bus! I have a wee-wee!
Stop the bus! I have a wee-wee!
And I'm bursting for the loo.

Stop the bus! I have a wee-wee!
Stop the bus! I have a wee-wee!
Stop the bus! I have a wee-wee!
Now Johnny has one too.

Stop the bus! I have a wee-wee!
Stop the bus! I have a wee-wee!
Stop the bus! I have a wee-wee!
And I can't hold it no more.

Stop the bus! I have a wee-wee!
Stop the bus! I have a wee-wee!
Stop the bus! I have a wee-wee!
Too late – it's on the floor.

A Young Child Learns to Write

IdontspacemywordsIcanthelpit
Istickthemtogetheryousee
Andteachergetsmadwhenheseesit
Cosnoonecanreaditbutme

New Words for Old

My little brother made a fart.
He didn't use that word but with all his art
I heard the little rascal say,
'I made a botty-burp today.'

Fluffy Licks Our Horse's Poops

Fluffy licks our horse's poops
And his mouth's all brown.
You'd swear, to look at that little dog,
'Twas the finest food in town.

Fluffy licks our horse's poops,
I don't know why he does,
And, when he's good and poopy,
He licks it off his nose.

Fluffy licks our horse's poops,
We just can't make him stop,
'Cos Fluffy licks our horse's poops
Every time he plops.

Fluffy licks our horse's poops,
Why, I just can't tell;
Fluffy licks our horse's poops
(Perhaps he likes the smell).

Fluffy licks our horse's poops,
He looks a pure disgrace;
Fluffy licks our horse's poops,
And then he licks my face.

A Young Puppy Explores the World
Beyond the Front Door
for the First Time

I went out into the Big
To have a look around,
I left behind my Cosy
And this is what I found:

It was too big to bite it,
What was I to do?
So I ran back to Friendly
And piddled on his shoe.

When the Car Killed Our Puppy

When the car killed our puppy
(There was nothing the driver could do),
All that was left upon the road
Was her blood and a little pooh;

So I got a pail of water
And washed the stains away.
I'll miss my darling puppy
More than words can say;

I'll miss my darling puppy.
No matter what I do
I'll never forget that pool of blood
And the little lonesome pooh.

I won't.

I'll never forget that pool of blood
And the little lonesome pooh.

On the Death of Missy, Our Puppy

I'll miss you scratching on the door,
Miss you playing 'round the floor.
I'll miss you, Missy.

I'll miss the way you wouldn't come
When I called – you turned you bum.
I'll miss you, Missy.

I'll miss your piddle, miss your pooh,
The cleaning up I had to do.
I'll miss you, Missy.

I'll miss those lovely, lonesome looks,
Even the times you ate my books.
I'll miss you, Missy.

I'll miss you more than any pet
I've ever had, could ever get.
I'll miss you, Missy.

I will.

I'll miss you,
Miss you,
Miss you,
Missy.

Goodbye.

The Christmas Puppy

She didn't yelp or wag her tail
Or lick your hand, not she;
She didn't sniff or nuzzle you
But looked suspiciously.

And so, while all the other pups
Were taken one by one
By new owners to new homes,
She was left alone.

They didn't take her, no, because
Of her different ways,
The kind of fear you sometimes find
In abandoned strays.

So, all alone, she spent the weeks
In silence, timid, still;
While all the other pups had homes
She had no home until

On Christmas Eve a lover came
In search of a surprise
For his love, his one true love.
He saw the puppy's eyes –

They won him with their lonesome look,
He picked her, trembling, up
And brought her to his lady love,
This little Christmas pup.

He brought her to his lady love,
A puppy, sad, alone;
On Christmas Eve the puppy found,
In the lovers' hearts, a home.

Carol

A hearty fire
Piled winter-high,
Stars of wonder
In the sky;

Turn out the lights,
The Christmas tree
Has light enough
For all to see;

And in the darkness,
All aglow,
We share this night
From long ago

With men and women
Of good will,
The child within us
Godlike still,

The child within us
Godlike still.

Christmas

The North Pole wind begins to blow
And with it comes the snow! The snow!
The grass is white, it's starchy-clean,
The whitest white I've ever seen;
Dad complains of ice and cold
(If you don't like the snow, you're old);
The trees and thorns are ice-cream white,
Stars are diamonds in the night;
The turkey's plucked, the pudding's plummed,
Christmas cards are stamped and gummed;
I can't wait for Santa, who
Comes to good and bold kids too,
For Christmas is the time of year
That makes you good, oh! I could cheer,
For when it comes to Christmas Day
We show our toys and play and play.

Wetting the Bed

It's so embarrassing,
You wish that you were dead,
Now you're out of Babies
When you wet the bed.

It's so embarrassing,
You'd think you were still three,
Not a big boy out of Babies,
When you make your wee.

And there's nothing really wrong with you,
You're not bullied in your school
Or frightened of your teacher;
You feel an awful fool

Because it's so embarrassing,
Your face would turn all red,
If anyone found out
That you wet the bed.

(Except your mammy.)

A Young Boy Discusses His First Holiday in Tenerife

When we went to Tenerife
I piddled in the pool;
I really couldn't help it,
The water was so cool;

The swimming pool was crowded,
'Twas full as full could be,
And nobody noticed
They were swimming in my wee.

Nobody except me.

I hope no one swallowed it.

When Dan Got Diarrhoea
in the Pool

The teachers took us all swimming,
We went in the bus from our school,
But when we went into the water,
Dan got diarrhoea in the pool.

There was nothing he could do about it,
He felt such a terrible fool,
It just bubbled up through the water,
When Dan got diarrhoea in the pool;

And we had to get out of the water
And go back in the bus to our school,
We weren't too happy, we told Dan get a
nappy,
'Cos Dan got diarrhoea in the pool.

He did.

Dan got diarrhoea in the pool.

In the Chipper

I went into the chipper
To buy a bag of chips,
And the smell was so inviting
I had to lick my lips;

But then I saw the chip man
Picking his nose,
And I began to shudder
From my head down to my toes.

Oh yes! I saw the chip man
Stick his finger up his snout
And, instead of buying a bag of chips,
I ran out.

And I never will go back again
To the chipper down that street
'Cos it's chips with salt and vinegar,
Not snots, I want to eat.

It's chips with salt and vinegar,
Not snots, I want to eat.

And that's for sure.

Tongue-twisters

Tongue-twisters are a good game,
They make your tongue trip up,
They make your words get knotted
Like wool would by a pup.

Tongue-twisters are a good game,
The teacher plays them too
(They're part of the curriculum),
But I have one for you.

Here's my tongue-twister –
Are you ready? Here we go!
You must say it really fast,
You cheat if you go slow:

Kitty Shine sitting inside her shiny shop,
The more she sits, the more she shines,
The more she shines, the more she sits.

And it's great to get the whole thing right
To the very end of it
But it's a whole lot funnier
If you should slip at 'sit'!

Lonely Day

Sometimes I think that I'm no good
And everything is wrong,
The things I do are useless
And my happy song

Comes out sad as sad can be,
And even when I play
I'm lonely, lonely, lonely,
'Cos it's a lonely day.

Will You Be My Friend?

Will you be my friend
And take away the Lone?
There's no home but Empty
When you're on your own.

Will you be my friend
And take me from the Sad?
Could you be the one to me let in
And good me out of Bad?

Will you be my friend
And let me in your fun?
It's lonely, lonely, lonely
Always to be One.

Will you be my friend?

Hush-a-Bye Baby
for Katie

Hush-a-bye baby
On the tree-top,
When the wind blows
I won't let you drop;

Hush-a-bye baby
In mammy's arms,
Strong as they're tender,
Safe from all harm.

Hush-a-bye baby.

Nanas

Nanas gie you goodies
When mammies say they can't,
'Cos nanas always give you
Exactly what you want,
And mammies can't give out to them
'Cos they are very old,
And that's why they're allowed to be
Very, very bold.

Katie and the Dolphin

Fungi is a dolphin,
He lives in Dingle Bay;
I went with Nan to see him
In a boat today.

We sailed from Dingle Harbour,
The boat went up and down
In the big, big water,
And very soon the town

Was far, far, far behind us
And we were out at sea,
Hoping to see Fungi –
Would he come to me?

And I looked out at the water,
Hoping for a peek
At the funny dolphin
Who plays hide-and-seek

In the deep, dark water
With children just like me,
When suddenly Nana whispered,
'Look! Look Katie! See!'

Fungi was beside us,
He was jumping up, yippee!
Jumping high into the air
And plunging in the sea;

And he played with us a long time,
And it wasn't like pretend –
A real dolphin played with me.
Now Fungi is my friend.

A Baby Brother for Katie

The first time I saw Pa-Pa
I was very shy,
But before long I got used to him
And gave him for a toy

One of my own teddies,
I placed it by his head,
But he was very fast asleep
In his little bed.

Yes, he was very fast asleep,
I rubbed him once or twice
'Cos he's my little brother
And he's very nice;

Yes, he's my little brother
And we love him – yes!
But still I'm Da-Da's little girl,
'Cos I'm my dad's princess.

Other Gabriel Fitzmaurice books published by Liberties Press

Poetry

The Lonesome Road: Collected and New Poems

A Middle-aged Orpheus Looks Back at His Life: New and Selected Sonnets

Prose (as translator)

An Island Community: The Ebb and Flow of the Great Blasket Island

Lucinda Sly: A Woman Hanged

*

All available from www.libertiespress.com and Liberties Upstairs

@LibertiesPress
@LibertiesU
@LibertiesB